My Little Book of

Timber Wolves

By Hope Irvin Marston
Illustrated by Maria Magdalena Brown

Windward Publishing

AN IMPRINT OF FINNEY COMPANY
www.finney-hobar.com

One spring morning, a timber wolf sniffed her way around a hill with her mate.

She was looking for a safe spot to make her den. Near the brook she found an old fox hole.

SCRATCH!
SCRATCH!
SCRATCH!

The wolf poked her head inside. The den was small, but she could dig it out some more.

She dug a tunnel twice as long as her body. She hollowed out a round little room at the end where she could have her babies.

Back and forth her paws flew as she made the opening bigger.

The wolf pack stayed near the den waiting for the pups to be born.

They brought meat for the mother wolf to eat.

Inside the dark den, the wolf gave birth to five tiny pups.

Lick! Lick! Lick!

One by one she cleaned them with her tongue.

Since their eyes were not open yet, she pushed them toward her tummy.

She curled herself around the babies to keep them warm while they drank her milk.

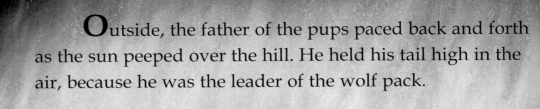

Outside, the father of the pups paced back and forth as the sun peeped over the hill. He held his tail high in the air, because he was the leader of the wolf pack.

The wolf tipped his head to listen to the tiny pups.

Back and forth he wagged his tail.

Inside the den, a tiny wolf was hungry. Or cold. The mother nuzzled its little face. *Grunt! Grunt!* The pup pressed against her.

Spring flowers were dancing in the sunlight.

But inside the dark den, a pup was squashed between the others and the wall.

"EEEEE EEEEE EEEEE!"
it whined.

It wriggled free and snuggled close to its brothers and sisters.

For two weeks, the furry pups ate and slept.

When their eyes opened, they crawled around the den on their fat little bellies.

One day the fluffy little wolves stuck their heads out of the den. They squinted their blue eyes in the bright sunshine.

They waddled along on their short, fuzzy legs.

They tripped over their big paws.

The wolves outside the den wagged their tails when the pups came out.

They played with the pups and licked them.

OO OWOOO OWOOO

The mother wolf howled. She was glad to be out of the den. Someday she would help teach her babies to hunt.

But today she trotted off, leaving them with a two-year-old "babysitter."

The babysitter lay down near the pups.

SWISH! SWISH!

He switched his tail back and forth.

The pups pounced on it.

They gnawed the sitter's ears. **THUMP!** They jumped on his back.

They pestered him until they wore themselves out and fell asleep.

That night, the members of the wolf pack ate together. They raised their voices together to howl. Then they curled up together to sleep.

The wolf pups spent the summer exploring outside the den. They wrestled. They played tag and T–U–G–of–W–A–R.

They attacked one another in fun. Their pretend fights helped them discover who was "top" pup.

Their father hid in the tall grass. They tracked him down and jumped at him.

When the pups grew too big for the den, their parents moved them to a grassy "rest area." They stayed there while the other wolves looked for food.

After hunting, the adults carried food back to the hungry pups. The pups whined. They nuzzled the mouths of the pack members to get the delicious meat.

The clumsy pups spent the autumn days eating and sleeping and playing. They stalked bugs and birds. And mice and rabbits. And anything else that moved.

They rarely caught anything, though, because they moved slowly.

The adults showed them how to hunt. They taught them to obey their leaders. They kept the pups safe.

Winter came. The wind whistled and blew the snow into huge drifts.

The wolves curled up together to keep warm.

They tucked their thick tails around their noses and slept until the storm passed.

When spring arrived, some of the three-year-olds left the pack to look for mates and to start families of their own.

The other wolves stayed around the den . . . and
listened for the mewing sounds of newborn pups.

DEDICATIONS:

For Arthur
– H.I.M.

For Jeff, Lisa, Mike, and Danielle
– M.M.B.

ACKNOWLEDGMENT:

The author wishes to thank Dr. Dorothy Hinshaw Patent, Ph.D., faculty affiliate, University of Montana, for checking the text for accuracy.

Copyright © 2003 Hope Irvin Marston
Illustrations Copyright © 2003 Maria Magdalena Brown

ISBN 0-89317-052-6
Second Edition, First Published by NorthWord Press 1997

This book is part of the My Little Book series.
For other titles in this series, visit www.finney-hobar.com or your favorite bookseller.

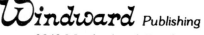
 Publishing
3943 Meadowbrook Road
Minneapolis, MN 55426-4505
An Imprint Of Finney Company
www.finney-hobar.com

Printed in the United States of America